Alexander Whyte

Father John of the Greek Church

Alexander Whyte

Father John of the Greek Church

ISBN/EAN: 9783337161958

Printed in Europe, USA, Canada, Australia, Japan

Cover: Foto ©Raphael Reischuk / pixelio.de

More available books at **www.hansebooks.com**

FATHER JOHN

OF THE GREEK CHURCH

an Appreciation

*with some characteristic passage
of his Mystical and Spiritual Autobiography collected and arranged by*

Alexander Whyte
D.D.

Oliphant Anderson & Ferrier
Saint Mary Street, Edinburgh, and
21 Paternoster Square, London
1898

Second Edition

Completing Fourth Thousand

Edinburgh: T. and A. CONSTABLE, Printers to Her Majesty

CONTENTS

APPRECIATION AND INTRODUCTION

APPRECIATION
AND INTRODUCTION

'They shall come from the east and the west.'—Our Lord.

FATHER JOHN, as he is affectionately called, is the great living pillar, and the far-shining ornament of the Greek Church of our day. And the Greek Church is the most ancient and the most venerable of all the Churches of Christendom. The Greek Church stretches away back in a direct and an unbroken line to the days of our Lord and His apostles. The New Testament from Matthew to Revelation was all written in Greek. And the Old Testament itself has now for more than two thousand years been far more widely read in its Septuagint Greek than even in its original Hebrew. The great Ecumenical Councils also all sat in Greek cities, and carried on their great debates in the Greek tongue. In no other tongue, indeed, could they have carried on their great debates; and in no other tongue could their great Creeds have been composed and handed down to us. The Greek tongue is by far the most powerful as well as the most exquisite intellectual instrument that has ever been perfected by the genius of man. And the finest use to which that fine tongue has ever been put has been the composition of the New Testament and the construction of the great Creeds of the Greek Church. To this day, when our Scottish children commit to memory their Shorter Catechism, they are already having their opening minds exercised in those deep distinctions and in those exact definitions that could only have been extricated and expressed in the Greek language. When they are taught to say, 'These three are one God'; when they are taught to say, 'The same in substance, equal in power and glory'; when they are taught to say, 'A true body and a reasonable soul'; when they are taught to say, 'In two distinct natures, and one person for ever,' our young people are already symbolising with Athanasius, and with Nazianzen, and with Cyril. They are being led back through their

own Westminster to Nice, and to Constantinople, and to Ephesus, and to Chalcedon.
The Westminster Larger and Shorter Catechisms
are a splendid education in Theology, and
especially in Christology ; in Church History,
also, as well as in deep and clear thinking, and
in correct and exact expression. Let those
noblest of all Church Catechisms always be
taught with all due learning, and intellect, and
reverence, and love.

The great and still lasting schism between
the Greek and Latin Churches was the result
of many causes and the outcome of many
occasions. Racial, linguistical, and geographical
causes and occasions entered into that great
schism : doctrinal and ecclesiastical causes and
occasions entered into it: but most of all,
religious and moral causes and occasions. The
conversion of Constantine entered into it.
The transfer of the seat of empire from Rome
to Constantinople entered into it. The Filioque
and other doctrinal and disciplinary contro-
versies entered into it. The production and
universal use of the Vulgate in the West
entered into it. But most of all, and most

disastrous of all, the bad passions both of the East and the West entered into it. Ambition, and envy, and jealousy, and suspicion, and prejudice, and fear, and ill-will all entered into it and exasperated it, and all these things have embittered and perpetuated the great schism down to this day. The fall of Constantinople before the conquering Turks led to the elevation of Moscow to its present pre-eminence over against Rome. What Jerusalem had been to the Jews: what Athens had been to the ancient Greeks: what Rome then was and still is to the Latins — all that Moscow at that epoch became and still abides to the Greek Church and to the immense empire of Russia. It was to the preaching of St. Andrew that the Russian people owed their first introduction to the Gospel. At the same time, ten centuries had to pass before the grain of mustard-seed that St. Andrew sowed so early had grown to be a tree great enough to cover that immense land. But at last, and as by a miracle, Russia was born to God in a day. And thus it was that in the year 1325 Moscow became what that famous city has ever since remained, the sacred seat of the Greek Church in Russia, and the proud and disdainful rival of Rome.

Every Church of Christendom, like every race of mankind, has its own special genius and distinct character. Unto the Jews became I as a Jew, that I might gain the Jews. To them that are under the law, as under the law, that I might gain them that are under the law. To the weak became I as weak, that I might gain the weak. So am I made all things to all men, that I might by all means gain some. The Gospel spirit runs itself into all the moulds of men and of nations. It submits itself, and resigns itself, and adapts itself to all manner of circumstances. Grant the Gospel spirit but love and prayer to live upon, and it will become anything you like to please you. And even in the supreme matters of love and prayer it pleases not itself but you, and your traditions, and your superstitions, and your prejudices to your edification. If you are a Greek, the Gospel will become Greek to save you. If you are a Latin, it will become Latin. If you are an Englishman, it will become English. If you are a Russian, it will become and will remain Russian.

And, accordingly, the Greek Church in Russia, like Russia among the nations, is the most conservative, stationary, and that to stagnation almost, of all the Churches in Christendom. The massiveness, the immobility, the inelasticity of the Greek Church in Russia is a proverb among all her sister Churches. No innovation has ever invaded the Russian Church. No development, either in doctrine or in discipline, has ever disturbed the venerable and vast calm of The Holy Orthodox Church. She is the true home of use and wont; she is the true harbour and house of refuge for all those who are determined neither to go forward nor to go backward, but always to stand still. 'The straws of custom,' says Stanley, 'show which way the spirit of an institution blows. The primitive posture of standing in prayer still retains its ground in the East; whilst in the West it is only preserved in the extreme Protestant communities by way of antagonism to Rome. Organs and all musical instruments are as odious to a Greek or a Russian churchman as they are to a Scottish Presbyterian. Even the schism that convulsed the Russian

Church almost at the same time that Latin
Christendom was rent by the German Reformation, was not a forward but a retrograde move-
ment, a protest not against abuses, but against
innovations.' The Russian Church is The One,
Apostolic, Holy, Orthodox, Catholic Church,
and all outside of her communion and obedience
are schismatics and heretics. We are accus-
tomed in the West and North to insolent
enough assumptions, and to lofty enough pre-
tensions; but the East looks down on us all
alike. We are all so many rank dissenters
and turbulent non-conformists to her. Rome
and Geneva, Canterbury and Edinburgh, are
all in the same condemnation to her. The
Pope is the oldest of her prodigal sons, and
General Booth is the youngest ; only the Pope
is by far the worse, in her eyes, of the two. The
first Pope, in her eyes, was the first Protestant.
He was the real and original father of all
liberalism in politics and all rationalism in
philosophy and in theology. In the words of
Canonist Theodore Balsamon,—'We excom-
municate the Pope for all his errors : and with
him, all the West who heretically adhere to him.

All the Westerns, therefore, are to be treated
simply as so many schismatics, and an
anathema must be provided for their abjuration.'
And that anathema is provided and pronounced
to satiety surely in every Greek Church on
every first Sunday in Lent : and that Sunday is
sanctified by the name of Orthodox Sunday.
On that orthodox and denunciatory day some
sixty anathemas are hurled at all heretics and
schismatics from Arius of Alexandria down to
our own day.   Anathema ! Anathema ! Anathema ! But on the other hand, for all the
orthodox Greek Emperors,—Everlasting remembrance! Everlasting remembrance! Everlasting remembrance ! Till I had gone to the
originals for myself I was wont to think that
the Commination Services of Orthodox Sunday
must be something altogether savage and wholly
insufferable to the mind of Christ. But I was
greatly disappointed when I felt myself forced
to surrender all my indignation and contempt
at the Greek Church on account of Orthodox
Sunday, and to admit that, with many imperfections from my point of view, and with many
things that, if I were their ecclesiastical and

devotional censor, I would strike out,—yet, with all that, there is a great deal on Orthodox Sunday that is not only as true as the word of God, but is also both tender and charitable, stately and noble, sweet and beautiful. Let us give the Greek Church, even on Orthodox Sunday, her full and even liberal due. Bless them that curse you.

It was his far-travelling missionary experience that transformed Saul of Tarsus into such a shining pattern of that divine charity concerning which he sings such an immortal song in his First Epistle to the Corinthians. As the great apostle passed on from land to land, and from one race of his fellowmen to another, he came to see that he must consult with them, and advise with them, and learn from them, and respect them, and love them, and generously acknowledge to them, and appropriate from them, all their native truth and goodness, if he was ever to hope to win them to the full mind of Jesus Christ. And all that, the greatest of the apostles more and more did, as his life went on, till he ended by standing, shall we say, next to his Master Himself both in wisdom

and in love. But our own Scottish Church,
even in her darkest days, was never more dead
to her Lord's command to preach the Gospel
to every creature than the Russian Church has
all along been, and still is. And the stationary,
stiff, and almost stone-dead state of the Russian
Church, in some respects, is not the outcome of
the somewhat stony Russian character only; it
is full as much the accumulated result of so
many centuries of a selfish and an indolent
neglect of one of her first duties to her Lord
and to the world. Had the great national
Church of the Russian Empire but devised
liberal things; had she been what so many
small and poor Churches have been both in
Scotland and in England and on the Continent
and in America; had she, with all her riches,
been a generous-hearted, self-denying, world-
evangelising Church—who can tell how all that
might by this time have been paid back to her
in spiritual life, as well as in ecclesiastical, and
political, and individual liberty? Her Latin
sister, with all her faults, did the noblest service
to her Master and to the world in the evan-
gelisation of England and Germany in the

middle ages. And even when she was nearest
to death in Europe, her missions to America
and China and India all proved that there was
still a living heart left somewhere in her for
Jesus Christ and for the spread of His Gospel.
And since the Reformation, and notably in our
own day, the missionary work of the Evangelical Communions is the brightest page of
this whole world's history since the days of the
apostles. The Church of Russia alone stands
all the day idle, while all her sisters are hard at
work in their Master's vineyard. All that
Stanley himself can say for her in this respect
is this: 'If the Russian Church is not a
missionary Church: then, neither is she a
persecuting Church.'

'Notwithstanding all that,' says Mr. Durban,
in a fine paper in the third number of *The
New Orthodoxy*, 'it must be manifest to every
open mind that we have here no decadent or
emasculated spiritual institution. A religion
which has vivified and resuscitated nations:
which throbs in the heart of one of the
mightiest and most rapidly advancing of
modern empires; which commands the spiritual

allegiance and gains the impassioned loyalty of the manhood of the Russian Empire, as no other Church does in any other land, is surely entitled to careful study by all those who feel interested in the comparative theology of the age,'—and, I will add, by all those who feel interested in far better and far deeper things than that.

Truly and intensely interesting as the subject is, and closely as it touches on the main theme of this discourse, at the same time, I cannot attempt to enter on a discussion of the great Office-books of The Holy Eastern Church; nor can I enter on the Public Worship of which those rich and elaborate books constitute almost the whole service. Even Neale himself acknowledges that he found the investigation of the liturgies and the euchologies of the Greek Church a task of the very greatest difficulty. 'The variety, the bulk, and the intricacy of the Office-books themselves; the number and the obscurity of the rubrics; the unwritten tradition that guides and adjusts all, and the knowledge of which is scarcely to be gained but by oral teaching; the abbrevia-

tions of diction; the extraordinary contractions
of words; the technicalities in the quotation of
Psalms or Versicles; the shifting backwards and
forwards from book to book; and the absence
of any one general rule for the concurrence of
festivals; these things form only one of the
many sources of our difficulty' in dealing with
the great unconsolidated and unharmonised
Breviary of the Greek Church. But while it is
absolutely impossible to reduce that enormous
subject into such a space as can here be com-
manded, there is one of their books of Public
and Private Devotion that well deserves to
be acknowledged in passing. The Slavonic
Service-book, entitled *Trebnik*, or *The Book
of Needs*, is an extraordinarily rich and beautiful compilation provided by the Greek Church
for the use both of her priests and her people.
The book gets its so expressive name from its
peculiar contents. This golden little book is
a *vade-mecum*, so to call it, which the Greek
Church puts into the hands of all her priests
and people to guide them in all the parts and
processes, exigencies and emergencies, of their
spiritual and devotional life from their cradle

to their grave. And, only take Mary out of it, and some other Greek intrusions ; only edit it up to our Protestant and Evangelical truth and taste, and it might quite well become a cherished possession for all our own household and personal needs also. And to those who can pass the mother of our Lord by with all the reverence and love that are due to her, and who do not indulge themselves over this and that stumbling-stone for our Western and Northern feet; to those who are determined to take no offence, but to seek their own spiritual profit only, *The Book of Needs* is a noble book, and a praise and an honour to the Church that has provided it for her pilgrim people. The whole book is of singular dignity, and, indeed, majesty ; but out of it all The Order for the Burial of a Priest stands forth as a service of the greatest stateliness and nobleness and impressiveness to the heart and the imagination of one Presbyterian minister at any rate. The present speaker is bound to say that he has found it a great education, and a great reward, to study both King, and Neale, and Palmer, and Blackmore, and Brightman, and Shann, on *The Book of Needs,* and on all the other liturgies and euchologies to which those learned men have happily given him such intellectual and devotional access.   But, perhaps, the very finest thing; the thing, at any rate, that I most enjoy in all the Office-books of the Greek Church, is The Great Canon composed by St. Andrew of Crete.   This devotional composition is called ' The Princely Canon,' and it well deserves its exalted name.   This so elaborate and so impressive devotion begins at the very beginning, and it takes the penitent through the whole of Holy Scripture, putting him into the penitential position and into the spiritual case of all the successive sinners whose sins are discovered, confessed, and forgiven in the Word of God.   The intending communicant comes down through all the recorded transgressions of faith and obedience in the Word of God, and at the name of each fallen forerunner of his he stops and says, ' I am the man ! ' And at the name of each saint, also, in the Old Testament and the New, he covers his face and says, ' Whose shoe's latchet I am not worthy to unloose.'   ' The Princely Canon ' is a splendid testimony to the depth of heart and to the spirituality of mind of its revered composer. This truly princely canon is sung with great appropriateness on the Thursday of every returning Passion Week.

But, all canons and euchologies of men apart —what about the open Bible? you will ask. Beneath and behind all her other likenesses to us and unlikenesses: apart from all other agreements and disagreements,—what about the word of God? Are the Holy Scriptures open to the Russian people, as they have been open to us ever since the Reformation? Or, does the Greek Church interdict, or at best suspect and grudge, the open Bible to her people like the Latin Church? Well, I am able to answer your solicitude in that matter in a way that will rejoice the hearts of all those who make that inquiry in the hope and prayer to receive a good answer. I put that whole question, with some anxiety, to my friend, the Prince Galitzin, who is both a loyal member of the Greek Church in Russia, and who at the same time knows intimately our best religious life in the West, both Roman and Reformed; and who

has, in addition, the fullest sympathy with those
who give the Bible its supreme and un-
approached place, both in public worship and
in private devotion. The Prince's memoran-
dum to me, after some passages on the old
Slavonic language as the official language of the
Russian Church, proceeds thus: 'The reading
of the Scriptures occupies so large and so important a place in the liturgy of our Church,
that every member who attends the services
regularly is sure to hear the whole of the
Scriptures read to him in a short space of time.
It is true that the Holy Scriptures were very
superficially known in Russia up to the com-
mencement of the present century; but that
was due partly to the great cost of the copies—
partly to the defective manner of the reading
of the Scriptures in public worship. But at
the beginning of this century, under the reign
of Alexander 1., Prince Galitzin, the minister
of ecclesiastical affairs, gave a great impulse to
the circulation of the Holy Scriptures. Seconded
by some members of the Society of Friends,
and by German pietists and mystics, the Prince
founded the Bible-work in Russia, and built

it up in the teeth of all opposition. A great impulse to the spread of the Scriptures at that time was given by the publication of a magnificent translation of the New Testament into modern Russian from the pen of Bishop Philarète Drozdoff. The Holy Synod also, the head and arm of the Russian Church, took the matter up, and did the greatest possible service to the Kingdom of God in Russia by placing the Bible within the reach of the poorest purse. For sixpence a well-printed and well-bound copy of the New Testament is now to be purchased everywhere in Russia. As to the diffusion of the Scriptures, that has been taken up most successfully by the British and Foreign Bible Society, and by a Russian Society for the spread of the Gospel. Both Societies have their agents and colporteurs who are general favourites and are universally respected. The great convents, also, are often most important centres for the circulation of the Scriptures. As for the colporteurs, they show a zeal and a courage that remind one of the enthusiasm of the Salvation Army. They may be met with everywhere urging people to become possessors of the pearl of great price. It is a rare thing to find a steamer or a train in which there is not one of those devoted men pressing the Word of God upon the passengers. The Bible Societies are not content with selling the Scriptures at a cheap price, they distribute the Holy Book gratis where the people are too poor to buy it.   For instance, at St. Petersburg a special agent is commissioned to distribute copies of the Scriptures to convicts and colonists on their way to Siberia.   Thanks to the Russian Bible Society, every posting-inn is provided with a New Testament on the public table.   It lies also in all the rooms of the best hotels.   The first book that the Russian peasant buys is the Bible.   It is the first book that he reads and reasons about.   And may God bless the good seed that thus falls on those simple hearts ! '

Such then, in much too short, is the Greek Church in Russia in which John Sergieff was born and brought up, and in which he is now an arch-priest and a main pillar.   I have instinctively and intentionally dwelt on the things of good report in that Mother Church, rather than on those of evil report. And who shall be offended with me for that? What kind of an unnatural son would he be who would not dwell on whatsoever things are venerable, and noble, and steadfast, and prayerful, and hopeful, in that apostolic Church out of whose roots his own Church sprang, and in whose ministry such a saint as Father John is now serving God? 'I am the son of a Sacristan of the province of Archangel, and I was born in the year 1829. From my earliest years my parents instructed me in prayer, and by their own personal example made me a religiously inclined boy. They took me regularly to church, and I loved the public worship with my whole soul, especially good singing. I passed into the parish school in the tenth year of my age : but I made little or no progress for a long time. I seemed to have no mind. I could not learn, though, all the time, I was a well-conditioned lad. Being so much put out by my want of success in my lessons, I prayed to God passionately that He would give me more mind and more ability to learn my lessons.

And all at once there came to me a marvellous clearing-up of my intellect, till I began to understand my lessons very well. And the older I grew the better I succeeded with my studies, till I was almost the dux of the whole school. And then in 1851 I was sent to the Ecclesiastical Academy of St. Petersburg to be educated for the Church at the cost of the State. I secured the post of clerk to the Academy, and I was able, out of my small salary of a pound a month, to send some help home to my widowed mother. Finishing my Divinity course in 1855, I passed on as priest to Cronstadt, and in December of that year I married the daughter of the senior priest of the place, by name Elizabeth.' (I here take in this from Stanley's first lecture on the Eastern Church. 'However fervent the Oriental Church has been at all times in its assertion of the ascetic and monastic system, yet among her ministers marriage is not only permitted and frequent, but in some orders of the ministry is absolutely compulsory. It is a startling sight to the traveller, after long wanderings in the south of Europe, to find himself among the mountains of Greece, and in Asia Minor, once more under the roof of a married pastor, and to see the table of the parish priest furnished, as it might be in Protestant England or Switzerland, by the hands of an acknowledged wife.') 'Of children,' Father John goes on, 'we have none, nor ever had any. In the very first days of my ministry, I made it a rule for myself to attend with the utmost possible earnestness to my work as a preacher and a pastor. I strictly examined myself as to my inner life. With this intent I took to the closest study of the Holy Scriptures; selecting from them what most concerned myself as a man, as a minister, and as a member of society. I commenced early to keep a diary, in which I set down my inward struggles with myself, and all my secret prayers to God, and all my gratitude for my deliverances from temptations, and afflictions, and all disasters. Besides preaching, from the very beginning of my ministry I tried to take the utmost care of the poor: the more so that I was one of them myself.' 'On the seaboard of the town of Cronstadt,' so a popular life of Father John runs, 'half a verst from the Cathedral of St. Andrew, stands a small grey house hidden from the view of the passers by a high boarded-up fence and a thick hedge. In this cottage lives the revered of all Russia, Father John Sergieff. The furnishing of his house consists of a bed with a hard mattress, a common table, a few chairs, and two or three presses,—this is all the furnishing and adorning of the house of the Cronstadt minister who distributes annually hundreds of thousands of roubles for help and alms to the poor. In the summer, even before the sun is up, and in winter, while it is yet long dark, Father John awakens alert, and serious, and self-entranced; and, after his ablutions, stands before his own icon and offers up his morning prayer. He altogether enters into his prayer; he passes into another world, and for the time forgets this earth. For about half an hour he continues in prayer, out of which he comes forth with the iron energy he has there put on, and with the fortitude of soul and body that carries him through another day, and with his eyes sparkling with an extraordinary light and love. Father John now departs to morning service in the church. But this is not so easy ; the gate of his house is already surrounded by a crowd of people, all but impervious, both of pilgrims from all parts of Russia, and of people from all around, seeking for his benediction, or just to see him. Advising, blessing, reproving, pushing aside, he sits down in his drosky. Although it is only half a verst to the church, Father John always drives, because, otherwise, he would not reach the church till the day was gone. At last the priest is at the altar, and the hour is six. He reads the Evangel, prays, and takes part in the praise. Deep, distinct, precise, and with a special reverence, his fine strong voice sounds out through the church, Glory to the Father, and to the Son, and to the Holy Ghost, and the crowd of people fall on their knees. The service finished, Father John will have twelve or fifteen visits to pay to sick and sorrowful people in Cronstadt ; several lessons to give to the catechumens and others ; a visit to St. Petersburg ; some tens of visitors waiting him at home ; and hundreds of letters to open and answer. And great part of these

are " requests for prayer " from far and near :
sometimes even from Germany; sometimes even
from England and Ireland. And so on to-
morrow, and the day after, year after year.'
And in all that, as a fellow-churchman of
Father John has said to me about him, 'everything that marvellous man touches he turns
to gold : from the dispensation of the Lord's
Supper down to teaching an infant class in
the Sabbath school.' 'Father John,' writes the
St. Petersburg correspondent of *The Times*, ' is
known and revered in every nook and corner
of Russia. This wonderful man, in the midst
of his Russian surroundings, seems to approach
in these days to the first apostles. He is
indeed a true physician of the Gospel. His
extraordinary healing powers, and the spiritual
and bodily cures effected by the reception
of his earnest consolations, are attested on
all sides by many sorts and conditions of
men. To those who believe in Father John,
and their name is legion, the age of miracles
is not yet over. Crowds press round him
whenever he leaves his humble abode, and
they are happy if they can only touch

the hem of his modest garment. Father John's life is one of uninterrupted self-sacrificing charity and Christian ministration among the poor, the sick, and the needy. Not, however, refusing his presence and prayers to the well-to-do and the rich, who send for him when other help fails, and never in vain, from all parts of the country. Steamboats and trains in which he travels to and fro are besieged with such crowds that the police have to protect him from their pressure. The report of his appearance in any house in St. Petersburg makes the news spread like wild-fire, brings throngs of poor people, running madly from all the adjoining streets, to get within the range of his healing presence, to receive his blessing, or to implore his attendance at the sick-beds of relatives and friends.' To this it may be added that the last Czar received the cup of blessing from the hands of Father John on his death-bed, and all but died in his arms. 'My people love you,' said the Emperor with his dying breath. 'Yes, they love you, because they know what you are. And I feel better when you hold your hands over me in prayer.'

Our own Archbishop Maclagan made a visit to the Russian Church in April of last year, and I take the following from an excellent account of the Archbishop's visit which appeared in *The Guardian* of May 26th :—

' But one more episode of the Archbishop's visit to St. Petersburg remains to be chronicled—namely, a visit paid him by the well-known priest, Father John of Cronstadt, the reputation of whose saintly life and extraordinary influence for good in all parts of Russia has already reached this country, where his book, *My Life in Christ,* has lately been published in an excellent translation by M. Goulaeff, preceded by a letter of dedication to our gracious Sovereign. On returning from a visit to the Hermitage picture-gallery, we found a telegram saying that Father John would call in the course of the afternoon, and it was evident by the groups of hotel servants already waiting about in the passages near our rooms that the news of his intended visit was already more or less public property. At last we heard a sort of rush in the passage, and one of the servants hurriedly looked into our sitting-room and told us that Father John had come. I went out into the passage and met the venerable priest, his face as usual calm, and lit with smiles as he made his way with difficulty through the crowds of hotel servants who were pressing round

him in order to kiss his hand or to receive his blessing. His influence in Russia extends far beyond the
Orthodox population, and I noticed that not only
several of the German Lutheran servants in the hotel
were pressing round him, but that even two of the
Mohammedan Tartar waiters from the restaurant were
seeking and receiving his blessing. Father John
stayed with us for more than an hour, and he and
the Archbishop carried on an interesting and remarkable conversation on the subject of the religious
condition of the poor in England and Russia respec-
tively, and more especially in the great towns, where
each of them has had such a wide experience. His
departure was attended in the passage by a similar
demonstration to that which had taken place on his
arrival, and it was with great difficulty that he made
his way to the lift, only to meet with a still denser
crowd in the street as he made his way from the
hotel to his carriage.'

But, with all that, Father John's biography,
and, especially, his autobiography, has yet to be
written. Even his diary, which he has been
writing every day all his life, is not a proper
diary at all. In his own strong and modest
words about it, his diary is only so many
moments of spiritual contemplation, reverent
feeling, earnest self-amendment, and peace with
God, and especially of prayer, all set down at

the moment, and the true value of which each several reader of what he has written is left to judge for himself. Now that is just what I have done. I have read Father John's diary over and over and over again ; and, along with it, all else of Father John's writing that I could lay my hands on; as also all I could collect of other men's writings from every quarter concerning him. And, judging him and his work for myself, and judging both him and it very highly, and both loving and honouring him in the Lord, I have been led to introduce him to my Classes as, to my mind, the greatest of living spiritual writers and a true scriptural mystic; altogether worthy to stand before us in our studies beside Behmen, and Teresa, and A'Kempis, and Rutherford, and Shepard, and Law, and all such-like devotional, experimental, and spiritual authors.

While the whole of Father John's auto-biographic diary is digested immediately out of his own deepest experience, there is, at the same time, a long catena of special experimental passages that runs all through the book, bind-ing it all together with the cords of a spiritual

man of the first order of such men. I have
an index of all those passages before me, all of
which are written in tears and in blood, in
truth and in power and in prayer, above all
the rest of this everywhere truthful and powerful and prayerful book. And, then, those
outstanding passages are all indorsed, as they
did not need to be, with this seal and counter-
sign, 'This is experience; this is my own
experience ; this is my own daily experience.'
And this continual stamp and seal comes in
suddenly, and with extraordinary impressiveness,
when he is warning and rebuking us, and, again,
when he is counselling and comforting us in some
extraordinary inward and soul-searching way,—
'This is experience ; this is my daily experience'
comes in,—I cannot hope to convey to you
with what power and authority this seal and
stamp comes in. When he is warning us, as he
often warns us, against the dark and cruel and
malignant passions of our own hearts ; when he
is imploring us to pray with our whole hearts ;
when he is encouraging and emboldening us
to rise up and repudiate the thoughts and the
feelings that the devil insinuates into our hearts;

when he is giving us his best pastoral advice
as to how we are still to sit at the Lord's Table
amid all fears and fightings of conscience and
heart; when he is back again with us at the
intensest and most penitent prayer ; when he
is assuring us, as if on his oath, that God will
always hear us on the spot when our whole
hearts cry for His mercy ; when on the same
page he tells us how, on such and such a date,
he called upon God in all the sinfulness of his
heart, and, as soon as he had finished his prayer,
peace and liberty established themselves within
him ; and when, after all that, his deceitful
heart would not return to God in abiding
prayer, such an abomination of sin and unbelief had it become ; when he is the most
plain-spoken of all preachers about the evils of
eating and drinking ; when he is ·pressing intercessory prayer on us, and the sure and im-
mediate recompense of intercessory prayer to
ourselves ; and so on through his whole book ;
it comes in, I cannot tell you with what surprise
and rapture of the heart,—' This is true ! '
' This is of experience ! ' ' This is my own
daily experience ! '   The absolute integrity and

the intense earnestness of the man ; his uttermost self-forgetfulness, and most of all when he is speaking most authoritatively to us about himself; his sweet and fascinating humility ; his hold of God; his hold of himself; his sure-footedness in the Word of God and in the heart of man ; all this—and his whole volume full of the same kind—makes John Sergieff to be a spiritual authority and a spiritual guide of the very first order; and proclaims him a mystical saint second, in some of those respects, to none of that noble family of the children of God.

Those great experience-passages are the source and the measure of the whole book. But for those great passages the rest of the book had never been written. And when they are once given, all the rest of the book is already given. And, especially, those deep parts of the book that deal with the Divine Nature ; and with the Divine Nature in its Oneness, Simplicity, Incomplexity, Uncompoundedness, Omnipresence, and Inwardness. Our spiritual experience of ourselves is the exact limit and the sure measure of our spiritual experience of God. Our spiritual discovery, and hold, and possession of ourselves exactly measure our discovery, and hold, and possession, and enjoyment of God. They are one and the same thing. And thus it is that our author continually insists on the oneness, the simplicity, the incomplexity, and the spirituality of our souls in the very same sense, and in the very same terms, in which he insists on the Oneness, the Simplicity, and the Spirituality of the Divine Nature. God is a Spirit, He is continually instructing and reminding us. A Simple, Incomplex Being. The Being, indeed, of all beings. The Almighty God is wholly present in everything that exists. He penetrates and fills everything full, according to its nature and its capacity. Everything that anywhere exists has its origin, its existence, its life, its preservation, and its well-being in God. He is infinite, eternal, unchangeable. Neither time nor space exists for Him. He creates and He sustains time and space only as an environment for His creatures. The whole mode and manner of the Divine existence is too deep for us. We cannot wade out into it. Who can imagine what it is to be everywhere, and totally, and wholly, everywhere? It is too high; we cannot attain to it. At the same time, all that is as old as Moses and David and Isaiah. Not Behmen, not Pascal, not Edwards, not Sergieff, with all the revelations of God, and with all the experiences of God's saints behind and within them, has gone deeper into God than David has already done in the 139th Psalm. *The City of God*, also, has it all in those well-known words : 'God is that Incorporeal Nature which is not contained in any place, but is all in every place.' It is but the epigram of another Latin Father : 'Deus ubique est; et totus ubique est.' And of yet another : 'God is a circle whose centre is everywhere and its circumference nowhere.' Only, the originality and the genius and the grace of Father John stand out in this, that he dwells on that, and returns continually to that, and carries back his readers to that, and all in the most sudden, startling, awakening, ennobling, and sanctifying way. Our God is wholly and totally everywhere; and therefore He is with you and with me in all His Godhead, and power, and truth, and goodness. And His equally Incomplex,

if Incarnate Son, is wholly with us also in all His
pity, and sympathy, and blood, and resurrection,
and righteousness, and intercession and media-
torial providence.   Believe, Sergieff continually cries.   Believe all that with all your
mind and with all your heart, with all your
understanding and with all your imagination,
and with all that is within you.   Work at that.
Labour at that.   Never leave off from that.
There is nothing else worth working at.   For
in God you live, and move, and have your
being, and your well-being, and in nothing and
in no one else.   ' This also is experience.'

Though I am here in the near neighbour-
hood of the Greek icons, I am not going to
enter on that stumbling subject.   It would not
be for your universal edification.   But if there
is any divinity student here who is strongly
drawn to a deep and comprehensive study
of the devotional life ; and of the manners and
the methods, the aids and the appliances of that
life, true and false, right and wrong, in all the
Churches ; let him read and digest all that
Father John has to say to him on that subject.
And then let him buy for a shilling Ralph

Erskine's *Faith no Fancy: A Treatise of Mental Images discovering both vain Philosophy and vile Divinity.* Between the Greek Mystic and the Scottish Calvinist, the tyros to whom Erskine dedicates his learned and able treatise will get both an opened and a deepened mind for all their days. All that can possibly be said for icons as an imaginative aid to faith is said in the most beautiful and winning way by Father John. And, then, all of that kind is put under the severest tests of philosophy and theology and Holy Scripture by our own Ralph Erskine in his most masterly and conclusive manner.

The great mystic's great chapter on faith and prayer springs immediately, and with immense impressiveness and fruitfulness, out of all that. 'This also is experience.' If God is indeed and in truth all that, then how easy it is for Him to give us all things we need when we take His ordained way of faith and prayer to receive them ! It is utterly unpardonable, it is absolutely suicidal in us if we still doubt, and halt, and come away from God with our hearts empty. Our Lord said it as plainly as even He could say it. Every one that asketh receiveth, and he that seeketh findeth.   Believe that you receive it, He said also, and you shall have it. Not to believe, then, is blasphemy against God.   It is making Jesus Christ a lying witness.   Only feel truly and sincerely your need of that for which you pray, and believe that it comes from God, and you will obtain anything and everything.   For with God all things are possible.   Whether you are sitting alone, or lying down, or walking abroad, or thinking, or writing, or working ; whether you are well or ill, at home or out, on land or on sea, be continually assured that God at that moment is wholly with you ; that He hears the finest breathings and beatings of your hearts ; and that He listens to hear and help you.   Has He not said to you that He waits for you to be gracious to you ?   Do you deny that ?   No, demands Father John, you must not either forget or deny or despair of that.   Forget, deny, despair of anything and everything but that.   Remember that for Omnipotence nothing is difficult, nor for Love a trouble or a task. All things, therefore, whatsoever you shall ask in prayer, believing, you shall surely receive.

He who doubts is severely punished for his doubt. For his heart is left of God hard, and cold, and dead in sin. On the other hand, all blessings ; all life, and peace, and power, and joy ; it all comes directly and immediately from God, and from God in reply to believing prayer. 'This also I have a thousand times proved to be truth in my own experience. My heart tells me so at this moment that I write. Thou, O my God, art an ever open treasure-house of all blessedness to me. Amen.'

I suppose it is all this : I can well believe that it has been fifty years of a life like this that has given this eminent man of faith and prayer such a name and such a power in the land where he dwells. You will say it is great ignorance and great superstition in the Russian people to run after any man as they run after Father John. And you will denounce it as great credulity in me, and great disloyalty to my Church at home, for me to admit that there is anything to be admired or imitated in any Russian archpriest. But I incline more and more, the longer I live, to be very easy of belief in the literal promises and strong assurances of

Jesus Christ, and in the boundless power of believing prayer. I am a miracle of importunate
prayer myself, as great as anything in Father
John, though I will never be bold enough to give
day and date for it in this life as he so courage-
ously and so eucharistically does. Try the
prayer of faith, and the literal word of Christ
yourself. You can lose nothing by it; and
you may—nay, to a certainty you will, gain
more by it than you can ask or think. 'This
also is experience.'

But with all that, and much more that is
equally precious and epoch-making for us in
Father John's autobiographic diary; at the
same time, that book, it must always be pro-
claimed, if only to propitiate people, is far from
perfect. 'Everything has two handles,' says
Epictetus; and Father John's autobiographic
diary is no exception to that true rule. For
if the diary has a rich handle for the teachable,
and the hospitable, and the thankful, and
the spiritual, it has also a protruding-enough
handle for the ill-natured man, and the impossible man to please. There are too many
motes, as I see quite well, in Father John's

Greek eye. There is far too much about the mother of our Lord, and about His saints, and about an extravagant and a superstitious faith in prayer, as well as about icons, and azymes, and such like. There are too many flies in the ointment, I frankly admit. And all that I contend for is only this, that the ointment, all the time, itself is good; is indeed of a peculiarly rich, and healing, and fragrant, and scarce kind. And, moreover, that the flies that have got into the box of spikenard can easily be separated out of it. At the same time, as another most true proverb has it,—one man's meat is another man's poison. And Father John has not written his book for all men; but only for those who are able and willing to profit by what he has written. He is bold to say as he hands us his great devotional and ex-perimental gift, 'He that is spiritual judgeth all things; yet he himself is judged of no man.' 'This man,' says Palmer, 'is in error only incidentally, and by no real fault of his own, but only through his unhappy tradition, while we are in the truth by no virtue of our own, but only through our so much happier tradition. And his zeal in communicating to us what he has experienced to be Divine truth is a personal merit and a praise to him. Whereas our want of a like experience, and of a will and a desire to profit by his, is a real vice and defect in ourselves.' Those golden words deserve to be printed at the head of every controversial page, and should be acknowledged and attributed to his honour everywhere as William Palmer's wise and irenical law.

If then that is so ; if all Father John's faults and errors, so to call them, are only of tradition and inheritance, whereas his attainments and his experiences in the Divine life are all his own conquest and possession; shall we not both believe and hope that to whom so much has been given, and such a good use made of it, far more shall yet be given and gained? Shall we not hope and pray, and both in love and honour, that Father John may yet become such a reformer in Russia, as powerful and as lasting, as Knox was in Scotland, and Wesley in England? Nicon had the making of a great reformer in him, and Lucar was the sympathetic corre-spondent and guest of Abbot and Diodati, and

others of the great Western reformers and
theologians of his day. But the time was not
ripe. Russia was not ready. To Lucar
especially our hearts and imaginations continually return. Had not the bowstring of
the Sultan cut short that truly apostolic life,
there is no limit to the service that Lucar
might have done for the Eastern Church of
his day. And all the past history of that truly
venerable but far too fossilised Church ; her
present position as the National Church of
Russia ; the growing power of Russia also
among the nations of the earth ; and then the
rise of such a man as Father John at the very
heart of that Church, will all make us wait and
watch to see if he is to be made of God that
great reformer and that great evangelist which
she so much needs. With his prodigious
popularity and influence with the common
people ; with his privileged access to the very
highest circles and personages in the Empire ;
with his so conspicuous loyalty and devotion
to his own Church and nation ; and with his
so essentially evangelical, and so profoundly
spiritual teaching and character,—is Father

John predestinated to effect the internal reformation and the spiritual quickening of the
Church and the people he loves so well? Dean
Stanley closes his brilliant lectures on the
Eastern Church with a fine page full of such
prophetical and wistful questions as these.
What will her future be? Will the Greek
Church venture, still retaining her elaborate
forms of ritual, to use them all as so many
vehicles of true spiritual and moral edification
for her people? Will she be able to cleanse
away the corruption and vice of the higher
ranks in Russia, as well as the deceit and rude
intemperance of the middle and lower classes?
The Russian clergy, as they recite the Nicene
Creed at the Lord's Table, always embrace one
another with a fraternal kiss, in order to remind themselves and the congregation that the
Orthodox Faith is never to be disjoined from
apostolical charity. Is there a hope that this
noble thought may be more adequately repre-
sented in their ecclesiastical development than
it has been in our own? Will Russia yet
exhibit to the whole world the sight of a
Church and a people understanding, receiving,

fostering the progress of new ideas, foreign learning, and free inquiry, not as the destruction, but as the fulfilment of religious belief and devotion? Will the Churches of the West find that, in the greatest National Church now existing on the face of the earth, there is still a principle of life at work, which is at once more steadfast, more liberal, and more pacific, than has hitherto been produced, either by the uniformity of Rome, or the variation of Protestantism? Such are some of Stanley's characteristic questions as he closes his classical book. Now, it is no more than the simple truth to say that these very questions, and many others more or less kindred to them, rose in my own mind continually as I read and pondered the life, and the experience, and the teaching, and the immense influence of John Sergieff. Jonathan Edwards read the news-letters of his day in order to see how the kingdom of God was coming all over the earth, and how the will of God was being done on earth as in heaven. Mr. Dobson, the Correspondent of *The Times* in St. Petersburg, first introduced Father John to the English people in a noble letter to that journal in 1891. And may we not hope one day to read in all our journals, that both by Father John's books, and by his preaching, and by his character, and above all by his prayers, the great Greek Church in Russia has again become all that she was in her Apostolic days, when as yet she looked forth on the world as the morning, fair as the moon, clear as the sun. and terrible as an army with banners?

SELECTED PASSAGES

✱ *The following passages are selected and arranged from*
'*My Life in Christ,' published in this country by*
Cassell and Company.

See at end of this Volume.

SELECTED PASSAGES

(1) *On his pursuit of Truth.*—Thou hast opened to me all the riches of faith, and of nature, and of the human mind. I have studied the laws that regulate the mind of man in its pursuit of truth, and the growth and the beauty of the languages of men. I have penetrated with some depth into the mysteries of Nature, into her laws, into the abyss of the creation of the worlds, and into their evolution and development. I know something of the wonderful history of our own earth also. I have acquainted myself with its different peoples; with its celebrated men, and with their great achievements. I have spent no little time and strength in the study of myself also, and of Thee, and of the way I must take to know Thee and to come to Thee. And I hope still to learn much more of all

that in the years to come. But, with all that, neither my mind nor my heart is satisfied : no, nor ever will be. My mind still hungers ; my heart still hungers and thirsts, and cries, Give, give. When and how shall I ever be satisfied? I shall be satisfied only when I awake with Thy likeness, and when the Lamb leads me to living fountains of waters. For He says to me, and I believe Him : The water that I shall give you shall be in you a well of water springing up into everlasting life.

(2) *On his own Heart.*—Do not give way to the dark feelings in your heart against your neighbour. For many dark and malignant feelings arise on occasion out of the bottomless depths of your heart. And he who has not learned how to subdue and expel these evil emanations will often become gloomy, and irascible, and melancholy, and bitter, and a great burden to himself and to others. When these abominable ebullitions are vomited up within you, force yourself to love and goodwill, to mirth even, and innocence. Do good and speak good concerning your neighbour, and your

wicked heart will be shut down, and all your evil feelings will scatter like smoke. This is from my own experience.

When malice against any one is roused in your heart, then believe, and say, and insist that it is the devil at work within you. Hate with horror the diabolical outcome of your own heart. Repudiate it. Deny it. Do not acknowledge it. Speak as Paul spake about it in The Epistle to the Romans. Say, it is not I that do it. This also is from experience.

I often oppose God and His holy laws. I am often unbelieving, selfish, proud. I often despise others, I often envy others. I am often avaricious, covetous, sensual, ambitious, impatient, irritable, slothful. I do not pity those who suffer. This, and much more like it, is my daily experience.

All my happiness and unhappiness is contained in the thoughts and affections and inclinations of my heart. If all these things are in accord with the will of God, then I am at rest. Then I am filled with Divine light, and joy, and blessedness. If not, I am uneasy, filled with soul-destroying darkness, heaviness, despondency. But as soon as I change the evil thoughts and affections of my heart into good affections; into affections like God and well-pleasing to Him, then I immediately return to rest and blessedness.

(3) *On his experiences in Prayer.*—Fervent, tearful prayer not only delivers the heart from sin, but it also cures bodily maladies and infirmities. It renews the whole being of a man, and makes him, so to say, born again, and a new creature. I speak from experience. What a priceless gift is prayer! Glory to Thee, The Only-begotten Son of God, who hath obtained for us the endless pardon of all our sins, and all kinds of access to the throne of grace!

As He hears every word of the prayer, 'God have mercy on me!' and fulfils every word of it: so, likewise, God hears and fulfils all the words of all our other prayers—the most personal, and particular, and peculiar, and secret; only ask in all the simplicity of your heart, nothing doubting. This is from experience.

I thank Thee, my Lord and Master, for teaching me how to pray simply and sincerely to Thee, and for hearing me when I so called upon Thee, and for saving me from all my sins and sorrows, and for afterwards directing all my ways. I called upon Thee in all my wickedness, and said, in the words of the Church prayer, 'O Lord our God, who grantest forgiveness to men through repentance. . . .' And as soon as I had finished this prayer, peace and exhilaration immediately took possession of my soul (29th June 1864).

During Passion Week the enemy hindered me just before the time of my ministerial work began by striking my heart with straitness, disturbance, and evil despondency. But I prayed with my whole heart, and with undoubting faith, to the God of my salvation, and said : 'O God, most merciful Father ! Thou spakest through Thine Only-begotten Son, Our Lord Christ, saying, Ask, and it shall be given you, and so on. Give me now Thy Holy Spirit, that my heart may be strengthened for the work of this week among Thy people.' And what happened ? I went through the

work of the week exceedingly well. I was
calm, kind, edifying, and did not experience
any oppression or uneasy hurry. I glorify the
merciful right hand of my most gracious
Heavenly Father. The longer I live and
work the work of God, the more I see that it
is ever necessary to strengthen ourselves before
every spiritual work by heartfelt prayer.

ON DELIBERATION IN PRAYER

During prayer it is absolutely necessary that
your heart should sincerely desire that which
you ask for : that you should feel deeply and
truly what you are saying. Pray slowly till an
echo comes back into your heart from every
word of your prayers. Yes. It is an absolute rule. Pray slowly, and with power on
every word. Pronounce each successive word
from the heart. Keep to the rule that it is
better to say five words from the bottom of
your heart, than ten thousand words from your
tongue only. When your heart is cold, stop
praying, and warm your heart by vividly repre-
senting to yourself your misery and your
blindness and your deadness ; and then go on

to pray slowly and fervently. The Lord will not forsake those who labour for Him, and who stand long before Him. With what measure they mete, it shall be measured to them again. He will reward them amply for all their pain and toil by sending a light, and a warmth, and a peace, and a joy into their hearts that the common run of men never taste. It is better to pray long and continually, no doubt, but all men cannot receive that saying. And it is better for those who are not yet capable of a whole life of prayer to offer short prayers, but always with an understanding and a fervent spirit. Let every praying man accustom himself to ask himself—Am I in real need of that for which I am on my knees? And do I, as I shall answer at the great Day of Judgment, really, and from my heart, desire it? Do I really wish it? and am I ready to rise off my knees and work out that amendment of life and that holiness of heart which are now on my lips?

ON ASSIDUITY IN PRAYER

Do not spare yourself, even if you have been toiling hard all day. Having put your hand to the plough, do not look back. God will not suffer in you duplicity, and easiness, and oversight, and self-pity. If you hurry over your prayers in order to give rest to your body, you will lose both bodily and spiritual rest. Oh! by what labour, and sweat, and tears is the approach to God ofttimes made and held fast! This is experience! The only means by which you can spend the day in holiness, and peace, and without sin, is the most sincere and fervent prayer as soon as you rise from sleep in the morning. Such prayer, and such prayer alone, will bring Christ into your heart, with the Father and the Holy Ghost. And their presence alone can fortify you against all evil, and guard and keep your heart. Why is long-continued prayer so necessary? In order that we may warm our cold hearts, and soften our hard hearts. Be sure of this, in spite of all sophistry, that time and labour are needed to soften and warm the heart. The Kingdom of Heaven suffereth violence, and the violent take it by force. Our Father knoweth what things we have need of before we ask them. But we do not know: and never will know but by much prayer.

This is experience, as all men of prayer will testify.

ON BELIEVING PRAYER

When you pray that your sins may be forgiven, strengthen your heart in faith, and put an absolute trust in His mercy. What are all your sins to God's mercy, whatever they may be, if only you truly repent of them? But it often happens that a man does not in his heart believe that he will be forgiven: counting himself outside of God's mercy. That man, in that mind, will never obtain forgiveness, even should he shed oceans of desponding tears. But always with a straitened and a burdened heart he will depart from the mercy seat, which is only what he deserves. 'Believe that ye receive, and ye shall receive.' Not to believe; not to be sure of receiving what you ask, and what God has promised, is a blasphemy against God.

ON IMMEDIATE FORGIVENESS

The Lord sometimes hears us instantaneously and unexpectedly. Often during the day I have been a great sinner, and at night, after prayer, I have gone to rest whiter than snow and with the deepest peace and joy in my heart. Let that be my experience at the evening of my whole life ! O save, save, save me, O Lord ! O receive me in that same way into thy heavenly kingdom ! Everything is possible to thee. And thou delightest in mercy.

Do not fear or forget to confess every night the sins into which you have fallen during the past day. A few moments of fervent repentance, and you will be cleansed by the Holy Ghost from every impurity. You will be whiter than snow. You will be covered with the robe of Christ's righteousness, and united to Him, and to the Father, and to the Holy Ghost.

After sin immediately say in your heart the Psalm, 'Have mercy upon me, O God,' and say the whole Psalm in and from your heart. If it does not take effect the first time, try again : only say it the second time more heartily, more feelingly, and then salvation will speedily shine into your soul. Be always contrite, and more and more contrite, the more you sin : this is the proved and experienced remedy against sin. If still you do not obtain relief, blame only yourself. It proves that you have prayed without contrition, without humility, and without a strong enough desire to obtain forgiveness. It shows that you do not see and feel your sin aright.

When you sin for the fiftieth and hundredth time in the day, and are seized with the most devilish despondency, say, from the depths of your soul with Metaphrastes : 'I know well, O Lord, that mine iniquities have gone over my head. But I also know that without measure is the multitude of Thy mercies, and that there is no sin that can overcome Thy loving-kindness. Therefore, O most wonderful Being, O Lord most good, do Thou show Thy mercy to me a sinner. Accept me as Thou didst accept the prodigal, the thief, and the sinful woman. Accept me, though in word and in deed, by my evil passions and brutish lusts, I have sinned without measure against Thee. Have mercy upon me, O Lord, for though I am weak and evi' I am still Thy creature. O

Lord, my God, I have put my trust in Thee.
Be Thou my Saviour, and loosen, and remit,
and forgive all my sins; and turn, and preserve, and deliver my soul, save me for Thy
mercy's sake.   Where sin hath abounded, there
let grace much more abound.   For Thou art
the God of the penitent and the Saviour of
the sinner.'   A hundred times a day.

ON THE CROSS

Look upon our Saviour's Cross, and contem-
plate Love crucified upon it for our salvation.
And think from what torments He has
delivered us, and to what blessedness He has
saved us!   He has snatched us from the
jaws of death and hell, and has brought us to
the Father!   O love!   O redemption!   O
indescribable blessedness!

After our Saviour's sufferings the Cross
became the sign of the Son of Man: that is,
the Cross now signifies our Lord Himself,
incarnate, and suffering for our salvation.   On
the Cross our Lord offered Himself as a sacrifice for our sins, and by it He has saved us

from the enemy: and therefore, we can never see even the sign and shape of a cross without thinking of Him, and doing Him reverence.

Why did the Holy Cross appear in the heavens to the Emperor Constantine? Surely in order to show him that our Lord Himself, and all His apostles and martyrs, entered into glory through the Cross: that the Cross is invincible victory; that all the enemies of Christ and His people will be vanquished through the Cross, and that all the oppressed and persecuted are under the protection of Christ and His Cross. And we also experience the effect of the invincible, incomprehensible, divine power of our Lord's glorious and life-giving Cross, and by its power we drive away from our hearts all evil passions, all despondency, all fear, and all the other snares of the devil. I say this sincerely, with full belief in the truth and power of these words.

ON THE CURE OF THE PASSIONS

Crucify them. Never indulge them. When you feel hatred to your neighbour: never utter it: never indulge it: never allow or entertain it. But set yourself to love him, and to say and do loving things to him. And, above all, pray for him. If you are of an envious heart, say and do benevolent things to the man you envy. When you feel pride, dash yourself and it to the ground. Tormented with malice and ill-will, follow after peace and love. The whole art of curing the diseases of the mind and the heart is by doing violence to them whenever they show themselves, and never, never indulging them.

ON INVOLUNTARY SIN

The sin to which we do not consent is not imputed to us. As, for example, involuntary distraction during prayer: impure and blasphemous thoughts: involuntary malice: involuntary envy : involuntary anger and ill-will. Our duty is to endure involuntary sin, which is our greatest cross, and to humble ourselves, and to be patient, and to pray without ceasing: Create in me a clean heart, O God!

ON THE TRUE SCIENCE

The science of sciences is to know our
passions, and to know how to conquer and
expel them. It is great science not to be
angry with any one, or with anything : not
to think evil of any one : not even if he
has done us evil : but to find an excuse for
him in ourselves, or in something else : it
is great science to despise gain, and praise,
and luxury : and to live temperately and
moderately in all things. And so on through
all the passions and affections of the heart.
Alas ! we have studied many arts and sciences :
but not yet our own hearts, and how to
keep them. Life is a great experimental
science. Nothing is more difficult than to pass
through this science ; this narrow way ; these
strait gates. And those who have not learned
either of their mother or of their schoolmaster
to have the faith and the fear of God, they
will find themselves unprepared to face life.
Often he who is dux at school, and wrangler at
college, is overthrown and outrun every day
in the race and wrestling-ground of life. He

is like a ship put out to sea without anchor, sails, or rigging.

ON THE EDUCATION OF CHILDREN

In educating children, we should attend first and last and always to the heart. For their heart is their life. But it is their life corrupted already with sin at its source. And society is corrupted precisely at its source through the want of Christian education. Neglect of the development, of the softening, of the radical amendment of the heart, is a thousand times more culpable in a parent or a teacher than neglect of mental education. For a mentally uneducated man deserves and receives our indulgence and our pity. But in how much worse an estate is he who, while full of a so-called education, is still more full of malice, and pride, and scorn, and envy, and gluttony, and covetousness, and all his other wicked passions ! The uneducated and plain man's simplicity, meekness, gentleness, humility, silence, and patience, —how much better are they than all our knowledge of letters and sciences, all our outward polish, all our feigned courtesy and studied expressions! Even sins themselves, being done in ignorance, are more excusable in the uneducated.

Parents and teachers! beware and be most careful not to let your children be wilful. Wilfulness is the root of bitterness in a young heart. It is the rust of the heart, the moth of love, the seed of much evil.

Look! are the pupils of our schools taught that which concerns them more than all else —prayer? Lord, said the disciple, teach us to pray.

ON OUR HOME-LIFE

Watch yourselves—your passions especially —in your home-life, where they appear most freely, like creatures of darkness in a safe place. Do not give way to vexation or irritability, else you will be mastered by it, and will fill your home with it. Our innumerable imperfections fill our home-life with endless occasions for vexation and irritation; and then, yielding to them, our home-life is soon killed dead. Our irritations and our outbursts only make matters worse. Be calm: you are not married to an angel. We all sin before we are aware; and we are all more obnoxious to one another than we know. Charity suffereth long, and is kind. Charity never faileth. Conquer everything by charity.

In all caprices, all offences, all manner of family unpleasantnesses, always sincerely blame yourself. Acknowledge yourself as the real cause of the unpleasantness. Say, ' It was all my fault '; and the house will be healed, and your first love and honour will return. Know nothing at home but more love.

ON EATING AND DRINKING

Avoid and escape a life of eating, and drinking, and dressing, and sleeping, and walking; and then again, eating, and drinking, and sleeping. Health and the belly are our two gods in this age, and I am a man of the age myself, and a great sinner in all these respects. To walk and drive for health, and to incite the appetite, such are the objects and aims of every day with many of us. Many of us—and I myself the first,—if we do not repent and alter our life, will be condemned for living like the beasts that have nothing but their bellies to live for. Tea and coffee and tobacco, even, pertain to drunkenness if indulged in for their own sakes, and unseasonably and in excess. Some men eat and drink and smoke continually. This is their diary; this is their whole life. Such a life is the death of the soul; and at a tremendous cost and cross to himself such a sensualist and glutton will ever be saved; he will know what it is to take up his cross daily when he begins to be a man of mind and heart; a man of God, and not of his bed and his belly.

When hungry, do not throw yourself upon your food. Eat slowly, and with sweet reflection on the goodness of God. Eat all the time the incorruptible food, rejoicing in Him who is the Bread of Life.

ON MAKING EVERY DAY SACRAMENTAL

On rising from your bed, say: In the Name of the Father, the Son, and the Holy Ghost, I begin this new day. When I awake I am still with Thee; and I shall be satisfied when I awake with Thy righteousness, and with Thy whole image. While washing, say : Purge me from the sins of the night, and I shall be clean. Wash Thou me, and I shall be whiter than snow. When putting on your clean linen, say : Create in me a clean heart, O Lord, and clothe me with the fine linen, which is the righteousness of the saints. When you break your fast, think of the length of Christ's fast, and in His Name eat your morning meal with gladness of heart. Drinking water, or tea, or sweet mead, think of the true quenchings of the thirst of the heart. If you wish to walk or drive, or go in a boat somewhere, first pray to the Lord to keep this your going out and coming in. If you see and hear a storm, think of the sea of passions in your own and in other men's hearts. If you are a scholar, or an official, or an officer, or a painter, or a manu-facturer, or a mechanic, remember that the science of sciences to you is to be a new creature in Christ Jesus. And every day, and in every place, work at the new creation which you yourselves are. Working with all your might at your proper and peculiar calling,—work out your own salvation in every part of every day.

ON KEEPING THE HEART

Having Christ once in your heart, take good care that you do not lose Him out of your heart. It is very hard to begin again. Your efforts to get Him back will cost you many prayers and many tears. This is experience.

The invisible God acts on my soul as if He were visible and present with me; as He is. He is ; and He knows all my thoughts, and all my feelings, and all my desires. And thus it is that every inward slothfulness, stubbornness, wilfulness, or other wicked passion, is always accompanied by its corresponding punishment. If my inward inclination is away from God, and from His Holy Spirit, then my own wicked, bitter, unholy spirit fills my heart.

People irritate and offend you; treat you with easily evident ill-will and contempt. But you must not pay them back. Now is your opportunity to be gentle and meek, and full of

the mind of Christ. If you let yourself out of
hand ; if you are excited, and hot, and agitated
inwardly, you will be vanquished of yourself,
and will lose the inward battle that was almost
won. Be always calm, serene, simple, unsus-
picious, and kind-hearted, and you will have a
double victory, first over yourself, and then
over your enemy.

We must carefully watch our own hearts
every day, lest the tares of death—self-indulg-
ence, unbelief, envy, hatred, and what not of
all that kind—spring up to trouble us. We
must daily descend into our own heart to weed
it. Besides this, we must by every means
known to us fertilise it by prayer, and medi-
tation, and reading, and holy imaginations,
and never let our heart out of our sight. We
must remember that labour, and even toil, ay,
and even daily violence, are all needed to the
great task of subduing, and keeping subdued
and obedient, the heart. It is through much
inward tribulation that we shall carry our hearts
home to heaven.

Bring your heart to God in a morning and
evening sacrifice. Give up your heart wholly

to God. You do not know the blessedness
and enjoyment of that; nor the misery of
denying it. Renounce yourself absolutely;
and especially all your sinful inclinations.
Malice, hatred, pride, self-will, envy, ill-will,
avarice, covetousness, gluttony, uncleanness,
deceitfulness, slothfulness,—what a heart! what
a hell is every human heart! And continually force yourself to be kind when others ex-
asperate you ; to ask for them, and for yourself
toward them, meekness, humility, gentleness,
benevolence, generosity, disinterestedness,
abstinence, chastity, truth of all kinds, and
righteousness. It is difficult to conquer the
passions : impossible. It is to die. It is death
and burial, and you alive all the time. But
it can be done. By constant watchfulness, and
self-observation, and prayer, you and God in
and with you will do it. But not in a day ;
not in a year. But at last your heart will be
a copy of Christ's heart, and all your passions
at the service of God, as all His Son's passions,
and appetites, and affections were.

You say, 'What shall I do with such a heart
as mine is? For it sets itself in constant

opposition to everything that is true and good. It is full of unbelief. It is without God. It fails me in the hour of trial. It fears when it should be bold ; and it is bold when it should tremble. What am I to do ? ' Hate it. Kill it. Take it to the Cross. Away with it ! crucify it, crucify it ! And after it is crucified, and dead and buried, it will be raised again, a glorious heart ; the copy, and the equal, and the fellow of Christ's heart, for holiness, and beauty, and sweetness, and peace. You will then know, and not till then, what a divine gift the image of God is, and what a splendid possession to all eternity a holy heart is. That is what you are to do with your heart. And then you will say : Who is a God like unto Thee ? O the depth of God ! And above all, in the heart of man !

ON THE GOLDEN RULE

Love every man as yourself; that is, do not wish him anything that you would not wish for yourself ; think about him, and feel toward him as you would think and feel about and toward yourself; do not wish to see anything

in his life or in his lot that you would not
have in your own ; do not keep in your memory
any word or deed he has done against you, just
as you would like all your own evil words and
works to be forgotten; believe others to be as
good, and far better, both in their deeds and
in their intentions toward you, than you are
toward them ; and then you will soon see what
will come out of that golden rule into your
heart and life. What peace! what absolute
blessedness! You will be this day with Christ
in Paradise. You will taste heaven upon earth.
The kingdom of God is within you. He that
dwelleth in love dwelleth in God, and God
in him.

ON THE PULPIT

Our old man is constantly present with us,
tempting us, snaring us, corrupting us, destroy-
ing us. This is why we occupy ourselves in
the pulpit with the old man and his works.
It is in order that both we and our people may
learn every new Lord's Day to know ourselves and the dangers of our passions. And

F

it is that they and we together, and by the
grace and strength of God, may slay the old
man within us. This is why we do not take up
our time and thoughts in the pulpit with any
of the things of this world. They do not
concern us. They are irrelevant and imper-
tinent to us. There is one thing needful to us
there till it is accomplished. Thus we labour
in and for the pulpit that our people may be
taught to know God in Christ, and to love Him
with all their hearts, and their neighbours as
themselves. This is an old text, but it is every
day new and needful as ever, and more than
ever.

And, then, a preacher, as a physician of
souls, ought himself to be above his own
passions in order to have his hand in the
cure of his people. He ought to be skilful
and mighty in prayer and in all kinds of self-
denial. He ought to be above all worldly
desires and delights. He ought to be, he must
be, above self-love, and pride, and ambition.
That is to say, he must be deep in the Divine
Physician's hands, and under His regimen for
all these things himself, if he would work to-

gether with Christ in the hearts of his people. If he is to enlighten others he must be enlightened himself. If he is to preserve his people from spiritual and moral corruption, he must have in himself the true spiritual salt. Physician, heal thyself first, and then I will listen to thee about my sicknesses and my salvation. This also is experience.

My Life in Christ

Or Moments of Spiritual Serenity and Contemplation, of Reverent Feeling, of Earnest Self - Amendment, and of Peace in God

'Saying and doing always such things as shall well please Thee'
Prayer before the Reading of the Gospel at the Divine Liturgy

Extracts from the Diary of the most Reverend

John Iliytch Sergieff

('Father John')

of St. Andrew's Cathedral, Cronstadt, Russia

Translated, with the Author's sanction, from the Fourth and Supplemented Edition

By E. E. Goulaeff

St. Petersburg

Cassell and Company, Limited

London, Paris, and Melbourne

1897

Price Nine Shillings

Fourth Thousand. Crown 8vo, Art Linen. Price 2s.

Father John

OF THE GREEK CHURCH

AN APPRECIATION, WITH SOME CHARACTERISTIC PASSAGES
OF HIS MYSTICAL AND SPIRITUAL AUTOBIOGRAPHY
COLLECTED AND ARRANGED

By ALEXANDER WHYTE, D.D.

'The author has been able to go straight to the heart of things. He has only seen in Father John the mystic, the saint, the lover of souls, the lover of Christ, himself so beloved that healing powers are given him for men's bodies as well as for their souls. Father John is like unto the Curé d'Ars, but more manly, better taught, and one who lives as near to God.'—*Scottish Guardian.*

'The little book, breathing the broadest spirit of charity, has an appendix of selections from Father John's writings.'—*Christian World.*

'Gives an interesting account of the Orthodox Church, and of the way in which it excommunicates the Pope; but the subsequent notice of Ivan Sergieff shows that a man can be a saint without necessarily being a member of the Free Kirk.'—*Scotsman.*

'Dr. Whyte's facile pen seems to go on for ever, but somehow we never feel that he is writing too much, or that the quality is deteriorating.'—*Aberdeen Journal.*

'Giv s a sufficiently full account of his life, drawn from various sources—private letters among the rest—and appends a number of "selected passages" which will whet the appetite and send many of his readers to the work whence they are drawn.'—*Freeman.*

'Dr. Whyte introduces his appreciation by a learned dissertation, brief and admirable, on the history and present position of the Greek Church—which will be of great value to many to whom this most ancient of churches has hitherto been but a name. The extracts from *My Life in Christ*, which make up the volume, will make many of our readers, we doubt not, hasten to secure what is surely a remarkable work.'—*S. S. Chronicle.*

EDINBURGH AND LONDON:

OLIPHANT, ANDERSON AND FERRIER

AND ALL BOOKSELLERS.

Fourth Thousand. Crown 8vo, Art Linen. Price 2s.

Santa Teresa

AN APPRECIATION, WITH SOME OF THE BEST PASSAGES OF THE
SAINT'S WRITINGS SELECTED, ADAPTED, AND ARRANGED

By ALEXANDER WHYTE, D.D.

'Its author is a Presbyterian minister, but he has the Catholic quality that can recognise the good, reverence the holy, conceive the true, outside the limits of his own community. The book is one of a very remarkable series, expressing in a high degree what we have termed catholicity of mind.'—*The Speaker.*

'This appreciation takes the form of a lecture, and is full of interest.'—*Westminster Gazette.*

'The selections will come as a revelation to most readers, and cannot fail to lead to appreciation and a desire to know more of one who could write with such inwardness, yet absence of egotism.'—*Scottish Congregationalist.*

'By the light of Dr. Whyte's biographical labours the almost idolatrous veneration in which Santa Teresa is held in Spain, the land of her birth, is no longer a mystery.'—*Liverpool Daily Post.*

'His pen may be said to be dipped in love and veneration for his subject, and his language is graceful, convincing, and stimulating. The whole tone of the little book breathes kindly, Catholic, Christian feeling, and readers owe a debt of gratitude to the writer.'—*Scottish Guardian.*

'We feel that we have entered into a new world, where white-robed angels stand.'—*Expository Times.*

'By this work Dr. Whyte has done a real service, and one which multitudes of readers will warmly appreciate.'—*Daily Free Press.*

'As an introduction to the study of the life and works of one of the most remarkable women of any age, Dr. Whyte's monograph is admirable.'—*Bookman.*

EDINBURGH AND LONDON :

OLIPHANT, ANDERSON AND FERRIER

AND ALL BOOKSELLERS.

Fourth Thousand. *Crown 8vo, in Antique Booklet form, price 1s. 3d.*
Art Linen, price 2s.

Jacob Behmen: An Appreciation

By the Rev. ALEXANDER WHYTE, D.D.

'Dr. Whyte has written an admirable appreciation of Jacob Behmen. It is perhaps the best thing he has yet published, and only those who know something of Behmen will do justice to the care and thoroughness with which the work has been done.'—*British Weekly.*

'A most impressive and delightful exposition of Behmen's aims and aspirations and influence.'—*Presbyterian Witness.*

'Dr. Whyte is at his best, and most characteristic, in this charming lecture.'—*Sunday School.*

'As in the case of others of the great mystics, there were two sides to Behmen's doctrine, one of which is of doubtful value and of very mixed character. Dr. Whyte gives an excellent appreciation of the better side, and does ample justice to the deep, devout spirit and extraordinary genius of this strange seventeenth century seer. He does it all with the fervour of one in full sympathy with the mind revealed in Behmen's writings.'—*Critical Review.*

'The character of the great Mystic is limned with the hand of a master, and one feels a deep gratitude to Dr. Whyte for thus stripping the tag-rags of absurd tradition from the personality of one who, like Enoch, "verily walked with God."'—*Liberal.*

'It takes a great man to know a greater, and it is a tribute to the largeness of Dr. Whyte's own soul that he finds these men so noble,—Dante, Bunyan, Rutherford, Behmen,—and makes them seem noble to the smallest of us. This is only a lecture; but we all know Behmen now as we did not before, with all our reading in him and about him.'—*Expository Times.*

'An admirable little monograph by one who deeply appreciates the teaching of the mystics.'—*Christian World.*

'The best thing about Dr. Whyte's Appreciation is, that it is a quite simple-minded and successful attempt to give a popular presentation of Behmen and his philosophy. It is indeed perfectly clear and within grasp, and, at the same time, it is a distinct contribution to knowledge, having the literary touch of an elegant writer.'—*The Unknown World.*

EDINBURGH AND LONDON:
OLIPHANT, ANDERSON AND FERRIER
AND ALL BOOKSELLERS.

Fifth Thousand. Post 8vo, cloth extra, gilt top. Price 3s. 6d.

Bible Characters
Adam to Achan
By ALEXANDER WHYTE, D.D.

CONTENTS

EDINBURGH AND LONDON :

OLIPHANT, ANDERSON AND FERRIER

AND ALL BOOKSELLERS.

Twenty-first Thousand. Post 8vo, antique laid paper, cloth extra. Price 2s. 6d.

FIRST SERIES.

Bunyan Characters

LECTURES DELIVERED IN ST. GEORGE'S FREE CHURCH, EDINBURGH: BY ALEXANDER WHYTE, D.D.

CONTENTS

EDINBURGH AND LONDON :
OLIPHANT, ANDERSON AND FERRIER
AND ALL BOOKSELLERS.

Tenth Thousand. Post 8vo, antique laid paper, cloth extra. Price 2s. 6d.

SECOND SERIES.

Bunyan Characters

LECTURES DELIVERED IN ST. GEORGE'S FREE CHURCH,
EDINBURGH : BY ALEXANDER WHYTE, D.D.

CONTENTS

EDINBURGH AND LONDON:
OLIPHANT, ANDERSON AND FERRIER
AND ALL BOOKSELLERS.

Post 8vo, antique laid paper, cloth extra.
Price 2s. 6d.

THIRD SERIES.

Bunyan Characters

LECTURES DELIVERED IN ST. GEORGE'S FREE CHURCH,
EDINBURGH: BY ALEXANDER WHYTE, D.D.

CONTENTS

EDINBURGH AND LONDON:

OLIPHANT, ANDERSON AND FERRIER

AND ALL BOOKSELLERS.

Sixth Thousand. Post 8vo, antique laid paper, cloth extra. Price 2s. 6d.

Samuel Rutherford

AND SOME OF HIS CORRESPONDENTS

LECTURES DELIVERED IN ST. GEORGE'S FREE CHURCH, EDINBURGH : BY ALEXANDER WHYTE, D.D.

CONTENTS

EDINBURGH AND LONDON:

OLIPHANT, ANDERSON AND FERRIER

AND ALL BOOKSELLERS.

Small Crown 8vo, on antique laid paper, cloth extra.
Price 2s.

The Holy War.

By JOHN BUNYAN.

With Prefatory Note by the REV. ALEXANDER WHYTE, D.D.,
St. George's Free Church, Edinburgh, and Frontispiece by
MRS. TRAQUAIR.

"A most delightful edition of the *Holy War*, which will, we are sure, be warmly welcomed. . . . Nothing better in its own line could be imagined."—*British Weekly.*

"The issue of the present neatly-got-up edition offers an excellent opportunity for those who have not yet made its acquaintance to study this great Puritan classic."—*Christian World.*

"An exceedingly well-printed edition of a book which is second only in interest to *The Pilgrim's Progress.*—*Literary World.*

"A more pleasantly readable copy of this immortal romance could not be desired."—*Glasgow Herald.*

"Perhaps the most surprising thing about the book is its price. Such a book as this used to cost 5s. always."—*Expository Times.*

"Who, if they did but see it, would be without Messrs. Oliphant's dainty and cheap edition with its antique title-page, and its symbolic frontispiece, and its prefatory note by Dr. Alex. Whyte?"—*Primitive Methodist Magazine.*

"For book-lover and student we do not know of a more desirable edition of a work which is not the best of its kind in the language only because Bunyan also wrote *The Pilgrim's Progress.*"—*Westmoreland Gazette.*

"The prettiest little edition of this immortal classic we have ever seen."—*Methodist Times.*

EDINBURGH AND LONDON
OLIPHANT ANDERSON & FERRIER
And all Booksellers.

Uniform with Dr. Whyte's ' Jacob Behmen.'
Crown 8vo, in Antique booklet form.   Price 1s. 3d.
And in Art Linen.   Price 2s.

Thoughts on the Spiritual Life

BY JACOB BEHMEN

Translated from the German by CHARLOTTE ADA RAINY.
With a Preface by ALEXANDER WHYTE, D.D.

' The little book will form a fit and accessible gateway for those who wish to go up into the inner shrine of Behmen's philosophy and religion.'—*Sunday School Chronicle.*

'This outward objective, hurrying, worrying, generation greatly needs devotional reading such as this.'—*Witness* (Belfast).

'Miss Rainy has done a valuable service to readers of devotional literature by introducing them to the best thoughts of Jacob Behmen.'—*Dundee Courier.*

' It is well done, and it was worth doing so well.   Some of these sayings are very fine, though that is the least of the book, the knowledge of the man being far better.'—*Expository Times.*

'Choice and simple passages from the writings of the great mystic.   Miss. Rainy has made a good selection, and has rendered the extracts into very readable English.'—*Glasgow Herald.*

' The English is certainly good, and no one would know from reading it that it had not been written in English by the powerful thinker who composed the work from which it is taken.'—*Spectator.*

' The selection is an exceedingly useful one, and includes the evangelical portions of Behmen rather than the ultra-mystical.'—*New Age.*

EDINBURGH AND LONDON :
OLIPHANT, ANDERSON AND FERRIER
AND ALL BOOKSELLERS.

www.ingramcontent.com/pod-product-compliance
Lightning Source LLC
Chambersburg PA
CBHW020037030726
47499CB00007B/2475